大地的色彩
All the Colours of the Earth

SHEILA HAMANAKA

MANTRA   LONDON

Chinese Translation by Sylvia Denham

First published in 1994 by William Morrow and Company Inc.,
1350 Avenue of the Americas, New York, NY 10019.

Mantra Publishing Ltd
5 Alexandra Grove
London N12 8NU

To Suzy and Kiyo and all the other children of the earth

孩童散發大地的色彩 -

Children come in all the colours of the earth -

吼叫大熊和高飛鵰鷹的奪目褐色，

The roaring browns of bears and soaring eagles,

仲夏草坪的軟語金色

The whispering golds of late summer grasses

和落葉的噼啪土棕色，

And crackling russets of fallen leaves,

海濤捲起小貝殼的叮鈴粉紅色。

The tinkling pinks of tiny seashells by the rumbling sea.

孩童披著跳躍羔羊般的幼髮，

Children come with hair like bouncy baby lambs,

或輕柔似流水，

Or hair that flows like water,

Or hair that curls like sleeping cats in snoozy cat colours.

或卷曲如熟睡貓兒的鬈髮。

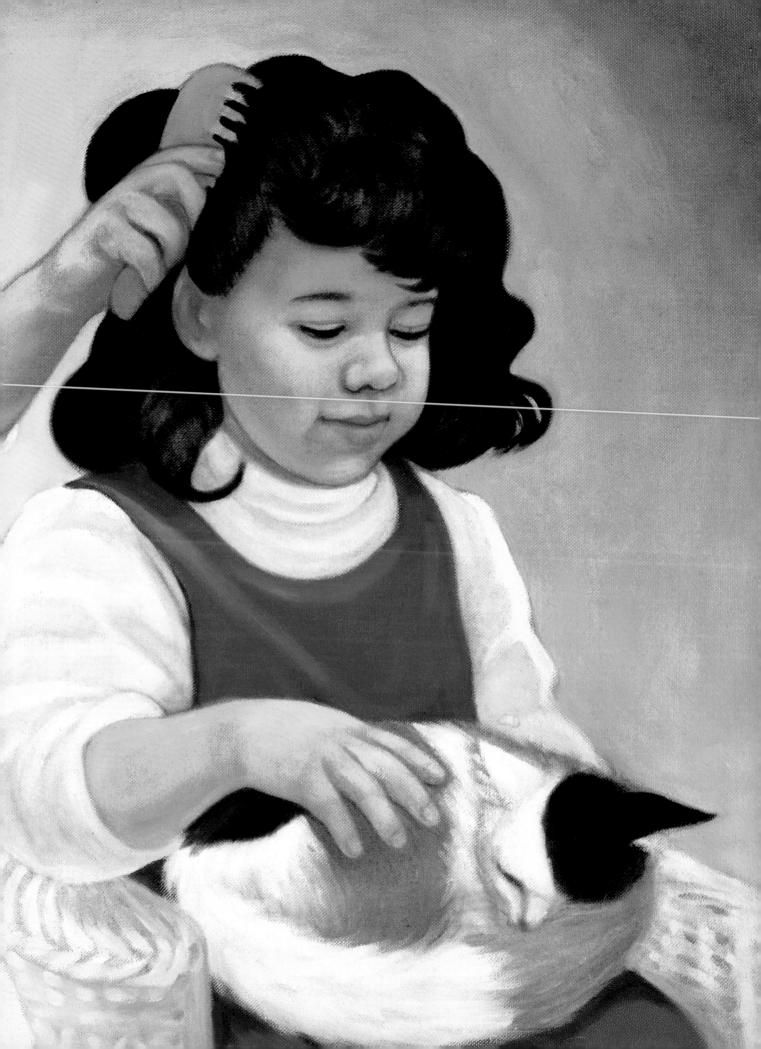

孩童散發繽紛的愛心，

Children come in all the colours of love,

是你我無盡影子的延伸。

In endless shades of you and me.

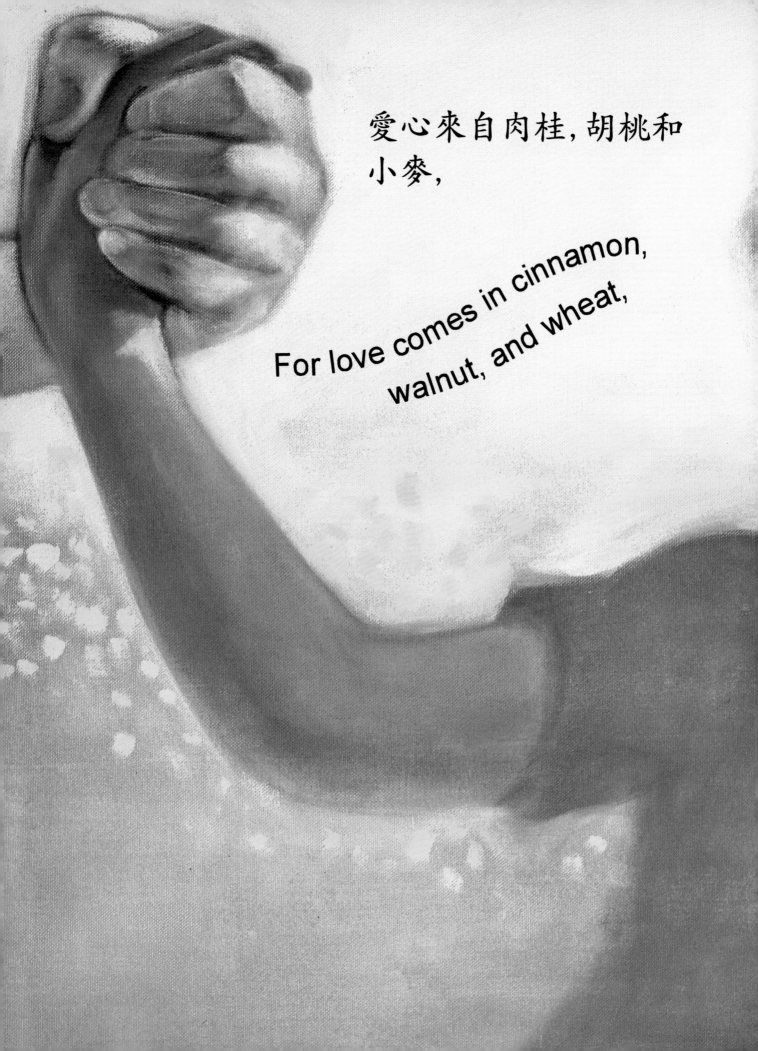

愛心來自肉桂, 胡桃和
小麥,

For love comes in cinnamon,
walnut, and wheat,

Love is amber and ivory and ginger and sweet

愛心是琥珀, 象牙與子薑及糖果,

猶如焦糖，巧克力和蜂蜜般甘甜。

Like caramel, and chocolate, and the honey of bees.

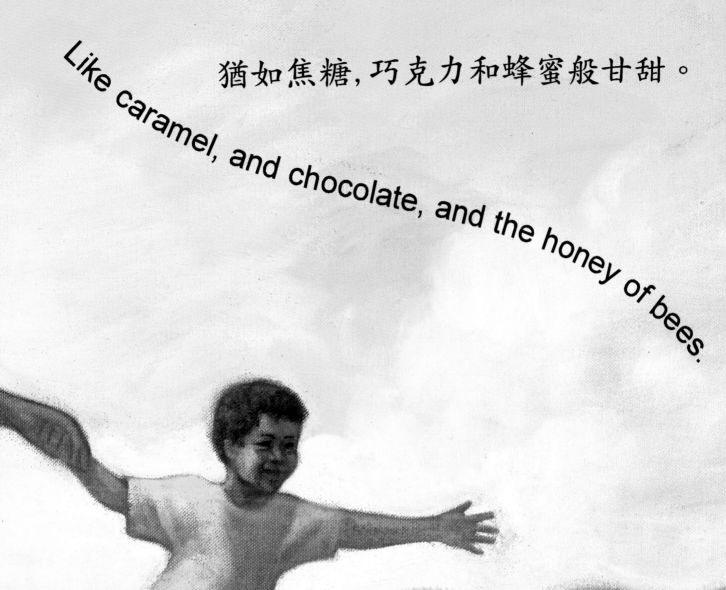

如豹子的斑點般漆黑，
如細沙般輕盈，

Dark as leopard spots, light as sand,

孩童嗡嗡笑語吻著大地，

Children buzz with laughter that kisses our land,

歡欣自由，像粉蝶飛舞似的陽光，

With sunlight like butterflies happy and free.

兒童散發大地,晴空
和碧海的各種色彩。

Children come in all the colours
of the earth and sky and sea.